Santa's Revenge

Santa's Revenge

Written and illustrated by James Rice

PELICAN PUBLISHING COMPANY
GRETNA 2005

Santa's Revenge

Library of Congress Cataloging-in-Publication Data

Rice, James, 1934-2004.
  Santa's revenge / written and illustrated by James Rice.
     p. cm.
  Summary: Santa Claus's face has lost its glow because of all the things the author has
put him through in other books, and so he takes his revenge.
  ISBN-13: 978-1-58980-250-6 (alk. paper)
  1. Santa Claus—Juvenile fiction. [1. Santa Claus—Fiction. 2. Stories in rhyme.] I.
Title.
  PZ8.3.R36Sa 2005
  [E]—dc22
                                    2004031083

Printed in Singapore
Published by Pelican Publishing Company, Inc.
1000 Burmaster Street, Gretna, Louisiana 70053

SANTA'S REVENGE

Santa Claus looked much too sad.
Now his face had lost its glow.
It started out with reindeer
Who were working much too slow.

He got a new team of gators
And bought him an old muskrat suit.
The suit was stiff and scratchy
And the gators were quite a hoot.

He moved his action to Texas
On a cold panhandle plain
And found a team of dumb ol' longhorns
Who were pure posterior pain.

He traveled on to the mountains
And got a team of big brown bears.
He came to wish those critters
Had remained at home in their lairs.

Still worse was a trip to Alabam',
Where he found a redneck with a gun.
At least two weeks Miz Santa passed
Picking birdshot from his buns.

Off to Ireland he went trippin'
With a donkey-pulled cart to roam
And a crew of naughty little elves
Who ate him out of house and home.

He went sailing on a silvery sea
In a rockin' rickety boat
Towed by a team of sea ponies.
They hardly kept it afloat.

One thing after another was
Adding up to too darn much.
How would he ever, ever pass
For a real Pennsylvania Dutch?

Teacher, doctor, fireman, and more—
Just where would it all end?
Whoever got it started
Was surely no true friend.

Said Santa, "I'll surely catch that villain—
For villain he must be.
Why else would he continually harass
Such a kind old gent like me?"

He knew where to look
To lay most of the blame
For burdening him down
With this unwanted fame.

He would surely teach a lesson
To that arrogant old man
For messin' around with Santa
And his ages-old workable plan.

Such forceful words from old Santa
You wouldn't believe that he'd say.
He chastised the old man soundly
And forthwith chased him away.

Now Santa's back in business
In the same old-fashioned way,
Making his annual rounds
With gifts, reindeer, and sleigh.

Old Santa is no longer sad.
His face has regained its glow.
He says, "Merry Christmas, y'all.
I've gotta get on the go!"